The Trial of Mother Goose

Ricky Kennison

AuthorHouse™
1663 Liberty Drive
Bloomington, IN 47403
www.authorhouse.com
Phone: 1 (800) 839-8640

Published by AuthorHouse 05/23/2017

ISBN: 978-1-5246-9324-4 (sc)
ISBN: 978-1-5246-9323-7 (e)

Library of Congress Control Number: 2017908164

Print information available on the last page.

Any people depicted in stock imagery provided by Thinkstock are models, and such images are being used for illustrative purposes only.
Certain stock imagery © Thinkstock.

This book is printed on acid-free paper.

authorHOUSE®

The Three Blind Mice claim to be eyewitnesses for the prosecution.

Mr. Duck comes forward and claims Mother Goose was with him that night.

Pinocchio demands to testify for the prosecution. He claims he saw the whole thing and can't tell a lie.

"It's a fishy story from the beginning," says Charles, but Moby Dick claims to know nothing. Moby Dick says it sounds like a whale of a story to him.

Prince Darling claims he was combing his hair and looking in the magic mirror and knows nothing.

The bailiff, Sarah, calls the defense's surprise witness, the Wizard.

Mother Goose's defense attorney is Perry, who claims he has never lost a case.

The Wizard exonerates Mother Goose, claiming it was a twisted story from the beginning and Mother Goose should be set free on Old McDonald's farm.

A chicken jumps up from behind Mother Goose and cries out, "Set her free!"

The prosecutor cries fowl and is forced to eat crow!

It's Thanksgiving all around!

The End

CPSIA information can be obtained
at www.ICGtesting.com
Printed in the USA
LVHW01s0916080917
547882LV00010BA/76/P